MARIA FINDS COURAGE

TONY & LAUREN DUNGY

Illustrations by **GUY WOLEK**

HARVEST HOUSE PUBLISHERS
Eugene, OR

To our children.
We pray you will find the courage
to honor God in everything you do.
Love, Mom and Dad

Cover design by Kyler Dougherty • Interior design by Left Coast Design

HARVEST KIDS is a registered trademark of The Hawkins Children's LLC.
Harvest House Publishers, Inc., is the exclusive licensee of the federally
registered trademark HARVEST KIDS.

MARIA FINDS COURAGE

Copyright © 2018 by Tony Dungy and Lauren Dungy
Published by Harvest House Publishers
Eugene, Oregon 97408
www.harvesthousepublishers.com

ISBN 978-0-7369-7323-6 (hardcover)
Library of Congress Cataloging-in-Publication Data

Names: Dungy, Tony, author. | Dungy, Lauren, author.
Title: Maria Finds Courage | Tony and Lauren Dungy.
Description: Eugene, Oregon: Harvest House Publishers, [2018] | Summary:
    Unable to join the swim team near her new home, Maria agrees to try soccer but has
    trouble summoning the courage to learn new skills and make friends with her teammates.
Identifiers: LCCN 2017038065 (print) | LCCN 2017047657 (ebook) |
    ISBN 9780736973267 (ebook) | ISBN 9780736973236 (hardcover)
Subjects: | CYAC: Soccer–Fiction. | Courage–Fiction. |
    Self-confidence–Fiction. | Moving, Household–Fiction. | Conduct of life–Fiction.
Classification: LCC PZ7.D9187 (ebook) | LCC PZ7.D9187 Mar 2018 (print) | DDC [E]–dc23
LC record available at https://lccn.loc.gov/2017038065

PRINTED IN CHINA

18 19 20 21 22 23 24 25 26 / IM / 10 9 8 7 6 5 4 3 2 1

Maria wasn't afraid of much. Spiders didn't scare her. Spooky stories made her yawn. But there was one thing that made Maria want to run and hide under the bed!

Maria's family had just moved to Trentwood, and Maria's parents thought the Trentwood Summer Soccer League would be a great place for Maria to make new friends.

But Maria wasn't so sure.

"Just go to one practice," Dad said.

"I loved playing soccer when I was your age," Mom said.

"But I've never played soccer before!" Maria protested. "Why can't I do swim team, like at home?"

Mom sighed. "I wish you could, but the summer swim team here is already full."

Maria tried a different argument. "Well, why can't I swim with my old team?"

Dad chuckled. "I think six hours is a little too far to drive every day for swim team. Come on, just give it a try."

On the first day of practice, Maria stood alone, watching the other kids kick a soccer ball around, laughing and shouting back and forth.

The longer she watched, the more nervous she got at the thought of meeting so many new people.

And what if she ran in the wrong direction?

Or tripped over the ball?

I'll probably be the worst player on the team, she thought.

A whistle blast made Maria jump. "Welcome to Trentwood Summer Soccer League!"

A man with a friendly smile and the word "COACH" on his T-shirt had blown the whistle.

"I'm Coach Tony, and this is Coach Lauren." The woman beside him waved.

"I know most of you from last season," said Coach Tony, "but we do have a new player this summer."

Maria's face felt hot as everyone looked at her. "Maria just moved here, so let's help her feel welcome!"

Coach Lauren stepped forward. "We're going to start today by running the skills course from last year."

Maria looked at the maze of cones, hoops, and nets set up on the field.
It looked complicated.

"The course helps you work on your dribbling and kicking," explained Coach Lauren. "Let's get started!"

With a cheer, the rest of the players jumped up and ran for the field.

Maria threw a panicked look at Coach Lauren. "I don't know how to do it!"

Coach Lauren smiled. "Just follow the other kids—you'll get the hang of it in no time."

But Maria didn't get the hang of it.

She tried to follow a girl named Keiko and copy her footwork, but Maria kept kicking cones instead of the ball.

She tried to hop in and out of the hoops as fast as three brothers on the team—Jaden, Jason, and Jalen—but her feet felt heavy and clunky in her new cleats, not light and quick like they did in the pool.

At the end of the course, each player was supposed to shoot a soccer ball into a small net. Maria kicked her hardest, but the ball went straight up and came down behind her, hitting a boy named Austin on the head!

Maria felt her face turn red as everyone giggled, and she wished she could disappear. She was sure no one would want her on the team now.

During the snack break, Maria sat alone on the grass, a little way off from the rest of the players.

Coach Tony came over and sat beside her. "Hey, Maria, how are you liking your first soccer practice?"

Maria looked down at her uneaten apple.
"I don't know anything about soccer.
I want to do swim team. I'm
great at swimming!"

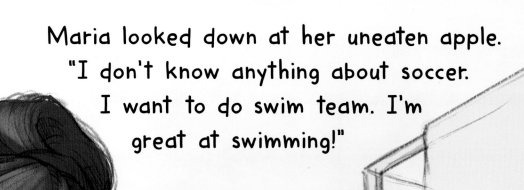

"Hmm," said Coach Tony.
"Let me ask you a question.
Were you born a great
swimmer, or did you have
to learn how to swim?"

Maria laughed. "I had to learn!"

Coach Tony nodded. "So there was a time when swimming was new for you, right?"

"Sure," said Maria.

Maria thought about that. "I guess you're right."

"Well, if you'd never tried it, you never would have found out how much you love it."

"You found the courage to try swimming even though it was new and probably a little scary," Coach Tony said.

"And that's how you know you can find the courage to try soccer too."

"But what if I try it and still don't like it?" Maria asked.

"That's okay!" Coach Tony said. "But if you don't try new things, you might miss out on something that could become your new favorite thing!"

"And if you never meet new people, you might miss out on new friends!" Maria said. She was beginning to get excited.

Coach Tony gave her a high-five. "That's right! And speaking of new friends..."

Maria turned to see Coach Lauren and a group of kids heading toward them.

"Hey, Maria!" said Keiko, dropping onto the grass beside her.

"You're ... "Coach Lauren said you might be afraid to c...
Cars... said Jason.

"Is it okay if w...
sit with...

Everyone laughed—Maria most of all. "Come on, where's your courage?" she teased. "Let's go!" And Maria ran toward the field with her new friends.

JOIN THE TEAM

THE TEAM DUNGY PICTURE BOOKS FOR
YOUNG READERS TEACH CHARACTER-BUILDING
LESSONS THROUGH THE WORLD OF SPORTS.

LOOK FOR MORE TEAM DUNGY BOOKS!

AUSTIN PLAYS FAIR

A TEAM DUNGY STORY ABOUT FOOTBALL